Planet Axul

Science Fiction

Written by:

Sofia Puga Velez

PROLOGUE

I awoke one day, not wanting to get up. I had dreamed something so vivid, so real, that it made me want to investigate, scrutinize and believe.

What could have been a presage, a *deja vu*, turned into an obsession to know what was beyond the rules, the established, beyond what they tell us, beyond what we have lived and absorbed throughout the years.

In this book not everything is real, and not everything is fantasy, which is good, because it awakens in us a curiosity that is vital to find a reality that satisfies us.

Some things not being real now does not necessarily mean that they could not become facts in a nearby future.

Since the times of Copernicus, those who would think differently were vetoed. We are conformed to others to do the thinking for us. It is time to wake up the child inside of us, the child that sees everything with astonishment, the child that does not understands about laws and rules limiting our minds.

I have to recognize that at the beginning I could not write without crying. Perhaps I had not found the maturity, innocence or strength needed. I can say that I have reached that maturity now when in writing the words are not painful anymore...

*"The simplicity of things
must call our attention more,
because you can see with
clarity and truth in them"*

INTRODUCTION

The first time I saw them, I thought they were part of a nightmare. I woke up stumbling, nevertheless stood up quickly. I was wearing what looked like a hospital gown covering me lightly from a cold that hit me to the bone. I knew then that I was a guinea pig for these beings, very much different from us humans. They were three of them and, although they provoke not fear in me, I did feel used and uncomfortable, which they knew because somehow they could read my thoughts. They calmed me down, I believe telepathically, and they began to tell me their story.

They came from our same galaxy, the Milky Way, but their stellar system was found on the other side, you could say almost in front of us. Their solar system was a spiral-ellipse, meaning that it was not flat, and their planets were ordered in different levels, some behind others, others in stair-like shape. It was formed by seven planets, but only one was inhabited,

Axul.

In that moment, another being just like them arrived. They told me that he would be my guide and would explain to me more in details why they came to Earth. Crion was his name and he began by telling me that there were more people like me in his ship. He took me there so that I could feel more secure. They gave me new clothes, then Crion came back for me to show me the rest of the ship.

Feeling a little bit better without the side effects of the anesthesia, or whatever substance they used to calm me down, I could notice the appearance of Crion.

His eyes were very big and round, yellow-colored. I could feel a sense of cold in them; they were like fish and cat at the same time. His nose was small, and his nostrils could open and close like manatees. His mouth was normal, it looked like ours. He had gills underneath his jaw, but they were closed and I could just make out three lines tighted to his neck. He told me that their heads and bodies were filled with something similar to scales before, but they lost them due to liquid they used to be able to travel.

Crion had been created in a lab, according to his own words. He had no parents and since he was a child he was raised by the elite forces of his people. The first moment I saw him, he appeared as if he was made out of stone, without emotions, but that was just an impression. Later on he will show me with facts that we should not get carried away by appearances.

He took me to a hibernation room where they still had bodies inside a capsule full of something transparent that looked like amniotic fluids.

Afterwards, he showed me a self-sustaining shed where they produce their food. I also too visited the dining hall and auditorium, everything impeccably distributed without leaving a single detail not designed for a specific purpose. At first glance, it looked like the ship was sufficiently big to shelter a whole city, and I was not wrong.

Later on he led me to a room where there were futons similar to a dentist office. I put a helmet on my head and Crion put one as well. That was, according to him, the best way to know what had happened in his world. All of his and everybody else's memories were stored in there, even before the journey started.

Table of Contents

PART ONE

PART TWO

Planet Axul

Science Fiction

Written by:

Sofia Puga Velez

Characters

Carmin Branco: Axulian, Tadeu's mother.

Crion Vriend: Immune Axulian, created *in vitro* in a lab, forged in the militia, of tempered nature, rough-looking, but loyal to his principles.

Eidan S. Laiton: Human, helped as a translator between Humans and Axulians.

Green String: Immune Axulian, doctor by profession, located in AXUL-Z (Sub), Nova's partner.

Isaac Matisse: Axulian, first Immune detected and treated in a lab.

Marena Paz: Immune Axulian, teacher by profession, located in AXUL-B (Bunk), Tie Jiang´s partner.

Mikhail Andreyev: Human, of Russian descent, astronaut by profession, his mission made him embark in the TERA-X ship, searching for a new Stellar System, Sara Smith's partner.

Nova Star: Non-Immune Axulian, stowaway in AXUL-Z (Sub) later adopted a life in the ship, Green's partner.

Sand Gray: Non-Immune Axulian, billionaire, located in AXUL-S (Sat), held the position of kitchen assistant in the ship, Tadeu's partner.

Sara Smith: Human, American scientist, contributed to decode the crop circles, Mikhail's partner.

Savia Flores: Immune Axulian, born in the countryside, her parents were sowers. Literally speaking, she is the most terrestrial of all the Axulians, even her scent resembles wet soil. She is located in AXUL X, assistant in the self-sustaining area, she takes care of plants and crops, Silver's partner.

Silver Blue: Non-Immune Axulian, (when he was born, it looked like silver sparkles would flash from his scales, hence his name). He is a scientist, his discover on the "Descent Theory" gave him a spot in the AXUL-X (Expl) ship, Savia's partner.

Tadeu Branco: Immune Axulian, kitchen assistant in AXUL-S (Sat), Carmin's son and Sand's partner.

Tie Jiang: Immune Axulian, engineer, located in AXUL-B, Marena's partner.

Planet Axul

PART ONE

AXUL

(Year 4380 - Planet Axul)

After a great search for solutions to the problems of Planet
Axul[1], peace was finally found for the wars. A change of
mind took place in the inhabitants of the different regions of
the planet. A calamity this big had to happen to realize that
there was no room for personal agendas and selfish
ambitions, if they wanted to exist. This happened after a
devastating earthquake desolated "Spring City", one of the

---

[1] **Axul:** 4th planet in System Cronos located at the other side of the Milky
Way

largest and most important cities in Axul.   Since then, everybody worked jointly to move forward.

Subsequently, more quakes had taken place in "Kysten Town" (another city located at the Southern Hemisphere), generating chaos, destruction and deaths. These quakes cause Axul axial tilt to move seven degrees. Since that day they realized that hurricanes shifted courses because of that change. Cities free from this phenomenon before were now exposed. Since they did not have evacuation plans in placed, they didn't know how to survive this sort of catastrophe.   Unimaginable cataclysms tested the will and survival of the inhabitants of Axul.

This apocalyptical shift in their lives had to happen in order for the planet's brightest minds to meet in a scientific council.

Out of them a young man, stood out, someone nobody knew about and had no convincing curriculum, a promising young fellow, unknown to everyone until that moment. His name: Silver Blue.

Silver had been researching the distance between Axul, its star Omega[2], and its cyclic movements. He would drew the conclusion that somehow the approach between the two was affecting the climate of the planet, increasing the global levels of heat.

This theory was very different from everything thought of until then. It knocked down concepts from old-school scientists, something unthinkable to them. They realize now there was no absolute truth in this matter.

After this concept was known, no blame was brought to the actions of the people when manipulating pollutant energy, a theory that has been discussed with greater strength; since there was no explanation for the natural disasters that took place with increasing intensity throughout the years. Even

---

[2] **Omega:** System Cronos star. There are 7 planets orbiting Omega

though the theory of global warming was rejected, people had to become aware that pollution is changing the environment and poisoning everyone's habitat in Axul.

The "Descent Theory" somehow explained the temperature increase when the distance between Axul and its sun Omega decreases. The Planet that has a tilted axis of twenty-eight degrees, it leaned twenty-one degrees now and started to fall somehow into a spiral orbit towards Omega. Fig.1

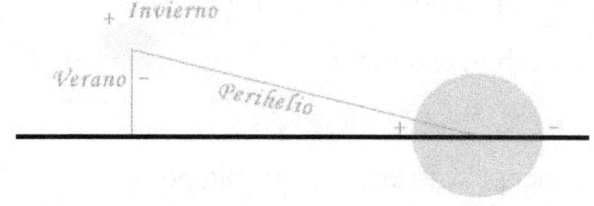

The inhabitants of Axul then realized that by helping each other, no minding of race or nation, was the way to face any disaster, whether internal or external.

This is how the Axulians started to build cities under domes. They started to feel the effects of the heat and its aftermath. People went blind because of the inclement sunlight, and when the planet hit the zenith point it was at it's worst. Skin diseases multiply in more than 1000% after the second semester of that year. This information is based on the history reports of the inhabitants of planet Axul.

Omega-Axul Attraction

Axul has two movements, rotation and revolution, and the newly-discovered descent movement.

The rotation movement is characterized by Axul rotating around its own axis. The second movement doing so around Omega, in elliptic form just like the Earth. But there is a mystery about the distance between Axul and Omega, according to its location.

The shortest distance happens when Axul is 133 million miles away, (we call it perihelion).

The longest distance occurs when Axul is 138 million miles away (we call it aphelion). Fig. 2

OMEGA-AXUL ATTRACTION

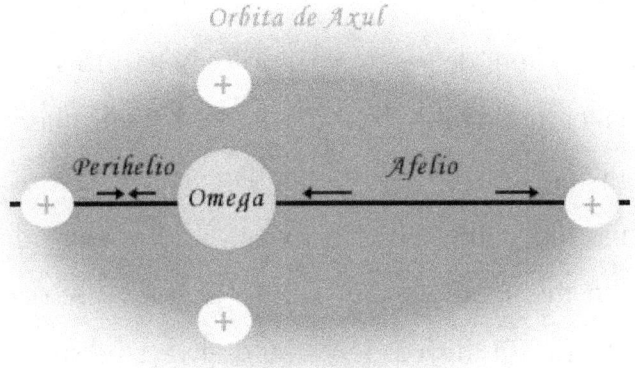

Fig. 2

It was known that this variation did not take place until all the astronomers and scientists agreed and drew the conclusion by the year 4381:

> Planet Axul leaned seven degrees in 4380, when a quake occurred in "Kysten Town". The previous year it had been twenty eight degrees and, even though this phenomenon did not repeat itself the following year, it is believed it will happen again, which would result in the end of the Axulian race.

OMEGA-AXUL ATTRACTION

The twenty one degrees obliquity tilts are no other than the gradient degree of Axul to Omega. This inclination makes the northern and southern hemispheres to be looking straight into its star Omega. If it was not like this and if the rotation axis would change direction, then the southern part would be the only one facing Omega. In this case, it would always be summer (hot) in the south, and winter (cold) in the north, this would produce a glacial period similar to what happened in the past, although the South Pole did not suffer this period.

Now, to corroborate the mystery of the different distances of Axul to Omega, we would give positive and negative sides to Omega, but instead of being in the south and north side, they would be located in the middle, on each side. So, when Axul's South Pole (-) and Omega's positive side (+) attract each other, in that moment the distance will be shortest. It will be

OMEGA-AXUL ATTRACTION

different when Axul's South Pole (-) and Omega's negative side (-) causes them to rejected each other. Fig. 3

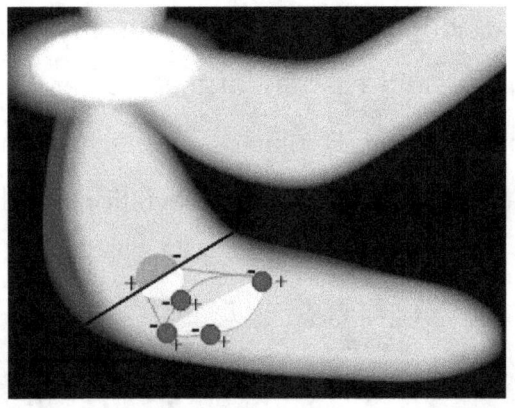

In this way it was demonstrated not only Axul's orbit, but also the orbits of the other planets. They belong to the stellar system Cronos, which is formed by six planets and one Exo-planet (Axul), giving a total of seven planets. Although they were not always seven. There was once one more planet, which was located in the sixth position. But an asteroid crashed it, turning it into star dust and waste in the strip or belt of asteroids that still orbits around Omega, called "K-PLUM".

It was also observed that planet Solenoid[3], the closest to Omega, was about to disappear, absorbed by Omega's magnetism. Solenoid has one of the strangest orbits, totally different from the other planets. This is what we call eccentricity on Earth because of its deviation of orbit. Fig. 4

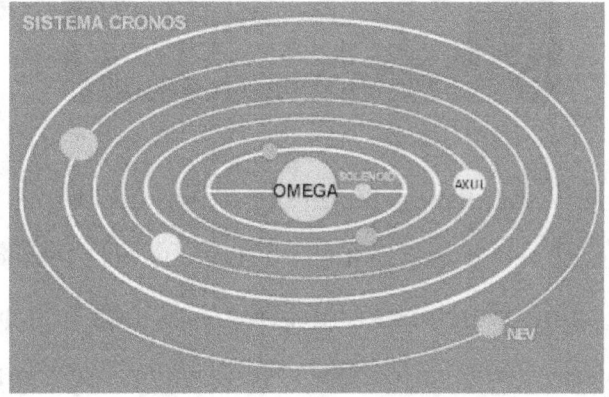

---

[3] **Solenoid:** 1st Planet of Cronos Stellar System

OMEGA-AXUL ATTRACTION

After realizing that every now and then Axul was getting closer to Omega, the fourth planet would have the same end as Solenoid. Scientists calculated and dated the end of planet Axul to happen in the year 4441.

By this time, every form of life would have been extinguished in Axul. So it was needed to act immediately if they wanted to have any hope for their race in the Universe.

Another theory emerged in the Scientific Community, it could be that apart from descending, there was an attraction towards Omega's center. This could be the worst case scenario, since years would become shorter and therefore it would take less time for the planet to collapse.

Escape Plan

(Year 4381 - Planet Axul)

Escape plans were designed, but none of them were conclusive in the beginning. The following year, Scientists realized that they were working against the clock, since temperatures had reached three digits in Fahrenheit scale, breaking all records.

They understood that the problem was just around the corner. The North Pole magnetism had moved from west to east, and there was a decrease in the planet's magnetic fields, which was a protecting shield from Omega's radiation. Without this shield planet Axul would dry out, the atmosphere would be lost, and it would be the end of life in the stellar system Cronos.

ESCAPE PLAN

A precession movement, a change in the orientation of the rotational axis would make Axul's magnetism became slower. When it stops completely, it would cause the winds and tides to turn to the opposite side, causing catastrophes in the four cardinal points. A huge wave would cover the planet creating hurricanes at a global scale destroying everything on its path.

Solutions were suggested, they recruited "the Immunes", people with high levels of immunity. Since it is better not to put all the eggs in one basket, five plans were accepted :

Plan A:

To build bunkers in the deep foundations of high-altitude Mountains, because they would be more secure during tectonic movements.

Plan B:

To build a submarine capable to stand pressure and high

temperatures. A huge global tsunami would be able to destroy life in Axul, but perhaps underwater there may be a chance of survival.

Plan C:

To build a spaceship to orbit around Axul, opposite to Omega. If everything describe here happens in the planet, this would not affect a satellite many miles away.

Plan D:

To populate the neighboring planet "Nev[4]", the farthest from Omega. It would be a temporary solution, because after all it would have the same ending as Axul, it will only give them more time for a last escape.

Plan E:

To build an explorer spaceship in search of new worlds. In

---

[4] **Nev:** 7th Planet of the Cronos system, it had been inhabited before until it lost its magnetism and towards the end also its atmosphere.

the end this would be a long-term solution, when there is no possibility of habitat in the known world.

In each exposed solutions there was a common denominator: to save the Axulian race at all costs.

When news about the catastrophe was known by Axulians, panic overtook the whole planet. Mayhem took place, everyone wanted a spot on the different ships. People fighting with each other, looting was rampant, even though they knew not everyone would escape a catastrophe of such dimensions, they thought that by having food and a hiding place in underground caves they could live longer. People would enroll in the army with the hopes of being one of the chosen ones to board a ship. Nevertheless, nobody knew where the ships were located. Government's officials hid the information about the ships and where the bunkers were being built.

Disaster Prevention

After having thrown overboard all speculations on global warming, they were focusing on giving a solution to the problem ahead of them. Emphasis was also given to personal and global change, especially on the respect of their surroundings, to raise awareness and make peace with Mother Nature, even during the end of times.

Time passed and there has been a transition towards the use of clean energy that won't poison the habitat of the living creatures of Axul. If a leakage were to happen, they would have a radioactive atmosphere were life would be impossible. What I do not understand is why they waited until the last moment to make these type of changes? Having a solution in their hands, they played the Russian roulette for all these past years.

DISASTER PREVENTION

While everything planned was taking shape the thermometer reached its highest point. Crops went to waste, and Axul's magnetism was almost non-existent. The end time was almost here.

Security patrols would escort and fly over the designated areas where they would pick up those who would inhabit the survival locations (meaning the Immunes). Many transportation buses were assaulted by citizens in aims of some hope. So instead of buses, it was decided to send recruitment ships to specific locations.

The Immunes
(Year 4237 - Planet Axul)

Isaac Matisse was born in Spring City. He was a baby like any other, even in his infancy you could not perceive any singularity. His adolescent life was quiet, he was passive in nature and sensitive at heart. He did not understand many things, yet he did not seek to explain or define.

When he was twenty years old, he suffered from a high fever that had a reaction on his brain and all of his body. After this incident, he was never the same.

He never got a fever in his life again. His reflexes were sharp, catlike reflexes, as if he could know ahead of time if something was going to hit the floor, he could grab whatever that was. His muscles developed so much that it seems as if he was a body builder, yet he was so clueless to boast about that unusual gift.

He could learn very easily. Somehow the fever had changed permanently his way of perceiving things and how he would react towards them.

Everyone would think that these qualities were a gift. Isaac, however, felt different and began to isolate himself. He would try to hide these abilities. He did not want to end up as a lab rat. In the end, however even against his will, they discovered the speed of his reflexes when hanging out with his study partners at a restaurant. Somebody sitting beside him strongly knocked over a bottle of spices, that the lid flew directly into Isaac's eye, who grabbed it instantly. Everyone was surprised about this incident, it was just the beginning for Isaac. Afterwards, he could not hide his abilities anymore.

They started to run some tests and, even though they treated him with freedom and respect, Isaac felt suffocated. He was declared the first Immune being ever since.

Later on, Scientists injected others with Isaac's blood, inducing some Axulians to become new Immunes. These new Immunes however, developed different kinds of immunity apart from Isaac's. A short time later and feeling intoxicated by the system, Isaac outsmarted his escorts and ran away from Spring City to never be seen again. He became a nomad someone with a continuous pilgrimage throughout his life. Nonetheless, the process had started and a new race of Immunes emerged spreading throughout the planet.

Almost a century had to pass before they were able to create the first ever lab Immune being; his name: Crion Vriend. He was the first created being to have complete immunity. But Scientists stop the experiments when they notice that Crion was missing a very important part that everyone else had: "Emotions".

THE IMMUNES

They didn't realized that in order to have emotions, these ones needed to be motivated, stimulated and by raising him as an experiment, his emotions were never reflected.

Not everyone wanted to be part of the immunity. Groundless rumors were created and people began to think that whoever got injected with this immunity would lose their soul. Since it was not mandatory, many people were not vaccinated; a decision they would regret at the end of times.

Resource Harvest
(Year 4382 - Planet Axul)

Authorities from every region gave all their resources they have to the Survival Council. They wanted to make sure the Axulian race would prevail. They would make the greatest effort to alleviate the effects of the catastrophe until the last moment.

So they began the harvesting of resources in collection centers, and the construction of the survival plans they had previously drawn.

From the beginning of times, people in Axul had gone through pandemics and catastrophes at different eras. Even at the present time they had come out ahead of all kinds of natural disasters. However, nothing came close to what was to come. A great scale extinction of every living being in the planet, even at the molecular level. They had to demonstrate their survival capacity once again.

They began to choose the best Immune people in every profession: scientist, doctors, engineers, etc. that had safely survived the different epidemics and diseases that had devastated the planet before.

Known as the Immunes, as told before, these were people that thanks to their high defense levels had not suffered from any viral diseases, carcinogenic or any other type. The idea was to keep the Axulian race alive, therefore, no one better than Immunes to endure the different levels of adaptation in any hostile environment.

Many Immunes were assaulted when the warning was given about the destruction of planet Axul. People would steal blood to inject themselves and be part of those who would be saved. But, since they were not treated in a lab, they were bound to die. Their own body would react against them, making their organs become solid as limestone. This would cause an auto-immune disease in them, very painful and fatal; that would consume them from the inside, affecting their central nervous system as well as other vital organs.

Finally, 230,000 people were gathered from every nationality, from even the ends of Axul. They were trained and informed about the exact day of departure: 07-30-4382.

When the day of departure arrived, the Immunes were nervous. They had mixed emotions, in one hand they want to go and at the same time it was hard to leave loved ones behind. It was really hard for them to be separated from their families and friends, a deep sadness invaded them. Nothing is more important for any rational being moved by his emotions than to be with his loved ones, even more so when knowing that they were not going to see each other ever again. For the chosen Immunes it was a time of recollection, a time of shared memories, they would take nothing with them only a small box of their memories; the ones that would give them the strength needed to continue their journey.

They gathered all the selected Immunes in their respective ships/bunkers, auditoriums packed to capacity. At the end I could notice a quote in every ship, rallying Axulians to be faithful and motivating them to be in tune with the Universe:

"Everything is possible until otherwise proven contrary"

Emotive words were given by a speaker and, although I only remember a part of the speech, it brought me to tears:

"...The most important thing is what we are bringing in our hearts, what we have cherished throughout the centuries, a carry-on, memories and the hope of shelter. In our imaginary luggage we would pack every lived moment. The supreme happiness of having known people who had shaped our destiny, have changed our own paths and had taught us the true meaning of love and respect. These are life stories never to be forgotten".

Mother Ship

The four mother ships were called:

AXUL-B (Bunker), AXUL-Z (Submarine), AXUL-S (Satellite) and AXUL-X (Exploration). Each will take 57,500 Axulians, they were designed in the following way:

One control cabin (for the captain and crew).

Ten public restrooms (with shared showers and toilets).

One auditorium (the one being in the center of the ship and it was a sort of roman coliseum. Seats were numbered and they will always be the same for each person. When departing or landing they needed to be in their respective seats).

One emergency room (medical clinic used by the doctors and their patients).

One boiling room.

One research room (used by scientist).

One self-sustaining area, very big for short-term planting and harvesting.

57,500 single beds (they look like coffins, one on top of another, in a very tight place).

57,500 compartments of hibernation (the quantity of compartments was the same as beds, but these had a viscous liquid with feeding tubes everywhere).

Plan A: Recruiting of Axul-B (Bunker)

Marena was a young 22-years-old. She had been one of the Immunes recruited to AXUL-B (Bunker). She was born by the seashore, hence her name. She had a gift for words, which helped her as a language teacher. She loved children and had a cutting-edge teaching method that was easily received by her students.

Once in the shelter, she became friends with everyone. She had a great understanding that her mission was vital and that she would drop everything to get to class before her students to get her classroom ready. She also volunteered as an auxiliary teacher for the adult classes in the afternoons (teaching was the thing she enjoyed the most, and she tried to transmit that to others).

The little ones were fast learners, the bunker would soon

become multicultural since there were people from different regions trying to co-habitat. So everyone would attempt not to forget their heritage and in that way their would contributed with their own culture without belittling other cultures.

The core classes could not be forgotten. They also include the new "Descent Theory" in the curriculum to help everyone understand why they were going through all these catastrophes in the planet, and to learn to survive them. Education became more open, to help them think for themselves instead of following strict rules that had them blinded for a long time.

In the bunker they did not have exterior news. They did not want people to be depressed by the sad news coming from the outside. Also, the inhabitants of the bunker would receive light therapy since Omega was an utopia for them at that moment. Somehow they had to look for a way to provide

PLAN A: RECRUITING OF AXUL-B

themselves with vitamin D.

Marena would never attend these therapy sessions, since she was always a positive girl, offering a smile to everyone that would need it.   She radiated her own happiness and optimism, as for her there was no better therapy than her colleagues and friends, with whom she would spend time after work. She herself was her own sun.

A foreign student arrived to her adult class. Tie was his name, a quiet guy, moody perhaps. She had not seen him before, and with her easiness of words she began to talk to him to get to know him better, by the end of the day they became best friends.

He worked in the environmental department of the bunker. His job was to keep track of the heat and cold levels to be exact, so that no toxic element would mix with the oxygen of AXUL-B.

PLAN A: RECRUITING OF AXUL-B

Little by little he would learn the other languages spoken there. He begun to feel better in his new environment and became more confident with everyone in the bunker. She had achieved a change in him for the better, but it had to pass some time before he realized all that Marena would inspire in him.

"D" Day

It was a summer morning at 4:44 in Spring City when the first quake was felt. Since the bunker was built on quake-proven piles that would move according to the tectonic movements, the quake was not as bad as it could be. This gave a certain degree of security to everyone inside.

The day that no one wanted to face finally arrived. There was a sense of fear, nostalgia, and melancholy in the air, sadness flooded Axul. The heat felt much stronger now, the air was heavy, the heat increasing as the minutes when by. A sense of sadness embraced Axulians from every race and region. At that moment tears came down my cheeks. As if knowing my reaction, Crion fast-forwarded the tape. The bunker gates were closed; the ships had departed three days ago.

In the bunker, everyone met in the central room and were told to remain calm. They gave them helmets and personal oxygen tanks in case there was a leakage and the air became very thin.

Most took their assigned seats, some people could not since the quake shuddered everything before they could make it there. This movement was even stronger than the previous ones, and many rolled on the ground. People screamed in terror, the power went out, fear overwhelmed them. Many were crying, moaning and feeling as if it was never going to stop.

The worst of their fears became a reality, there were fatal victims in their mist, and with the power out the fear was greater. It was not until everything calmed down that they realized the severity of the disaster.

At dawn, the bunker still didn't have electricity. Even though they were used to the absence of the sun, being without light felt like being blind. There was a question in the air, a claim:

"To think that the one that gives life once now takes it back"
(because of Omega and its effects)

As soon as he got up, Tie started to look for Marena. There was something about her that make him worry for her safety. He needed to know that she was alright.

With just a flashlight in his pocket, which he always carried with him, he gave into the task of looking for her and did not stop until he found her, still shaking and scared to death. He hugged her and then noticed his feelings for her, and how important Marena was in his life, what she meant to him, and how she had managed to break down his walls. At that moment, he did not say anything to her, because he felt dazed by what was happening. Also, he did not know how she would take it, so he decided not to say anything at all.

Raising from the Ashes

There was a lot of movement in Axul-B, this time it was not the quake, but people running up and down, helping those injured and cleaning up all the trash left by the quake. It was a great sight to see that at the hardest of times the Axulians showed the best in them. Everyone pitched in to bring Bunker city forward.

Little by little everything was put in place once again. Also the idea of getting out of the bunker was taking shape, but there were still lots of nights before they would be able to see the sunlight again.

They started by implementing the use of robots to be sent outside. These robots have helped explore other planets, but now they would become Axulian's lifesavers. They would pick up samples of air, dust and water to make sure life was possible again.

Meanwhile, Tie could no longer hide his feelings for Marena.

- Tie could you tell me when are we are going to stop wearing these oxygen masks? – said Marena.
- We are working on that against the clock. I came by just to see you for a moment. I have not seen you in three days. I have missed you – said Tie.

Marena looked at him, realizing his feelings for her. She felt confused and looked down.

- Don't worry Marena, I don't demand for you to feel the same – Tie whispered and walked away downcast-ed.

RAISING FROM THE ASHES

That night, Marena had trouble falling asleep. Something that was not there before had awaken in her, something she could not explain or describe, an urge to see him again.

The next day Tie did not show up at all, or the day after, nevertheless Marena knew that the environment had been regulated in the bunker. She also thought that perhaps he did not want to face her because he was embarrassed. So Marena went out to look for him.

- You have disappear from my life Tie and I have not given you permission to do that – she smiled.
- I have been busy working over here to bring oxygen to your lungs – Tie smiled back.
- Thanks for being my savior – both smiled.

She hold his hand as a way of letting him know that she felt the same about him. An innocent kiss sealed that moment in their lives.

Plan B: Submarine Journey

A submarine the size of a city was built, AXUL-Z. The reason was that if water is so abundant in the planet, any ship would be so minuscule next to the wide open sea. The sea was their main support system before and now it would be again, but this time as a safe survival mechanism that would offer them shelter, just like a mother's womb protects the baby inside. This solution would allow them to bet on the destiny of the Axulian race.

Green was a young doctor, a very gentle person with green eyes and good-looking, he was a gentleman. Ever since he was little guy, he knew what he wanted to be in life. This is the reason he graduated from medical school before the rest of his peers. Everything was working out for his future until

PLAN B: SUBMARINE JOURNEY

that ill-fated day when the news about the fate of the planet spread like wildfire. As soon as he found out the imminent destiny of the planet, as a good Axulian he applied so he could help everyone. He was one of the chosen ones to inhabit AXUL-Z, not only because he was Immune, but also to serve on board.

As with the others, it was hard for him to adapt to tight spaces and to the lack of sunlight. Soon they would lose their natural shine to become gray-like beings, but this would not affect their happiness for life. They had a natural seaquarium that somehow filled theirs lives with beauty. An unbreakable glass separated the underwater ecosystem from the Axulians. When they saw the variety of fish, they understood more than ever that they must respect live in every expression. It was easier to understand that their lives were also threatened by a massive extinction.

Breaking the Rules

Like the other ships, AXUL-Z was designed to be independent
and self-sustainable. All ships have same regulations: nobody
could take the life of another, and nobody would get
pregnant, since they did not know how long they would be in
there, and since they could not allow an over population
inside the ships.

A stowaway got in AXUL-Z, her cleverness simply was
rewarded by her acceptance to stay in the ship. After all once
the gates were closed nobody could get in or out. They did
not notice the new member until they started to give away
the cubicles and one was missing.

Her name was Nova. She was a very smart young lady, she
was not Immune, and with this she broke all the rules. She

had a gracious face and a friendly personality that made everyone love her. She did not have a college degree, however she had the ability to learn very fast, she would become a cherished person for them all.

The day that Green and Nova met, the ocean brightened up. A school of fish made its ceremonial appearance behind the glass. Something that looked like seahorses also arrived uninvited.

Both of them could not sleep that night, so each one headed to the seaquarium separately. Green found Nova looking carefully at the hippocampus. He approached her and said:

- Do you know the history of seahorses?
- Not at all – said Nova – can you tell me?
- Seahorses are the most loyal little animals in nature, every day they wander around coral, it is a routine that keeps them together forever. Then the female goes away, but comes back the following morning

for their daily routine. Also, their love is so strong that the male helps the female incubate their hatchlings and is the one who ends up giving birth to them – explained Green.

- What a great story – commented Nova.

- You are the girl who came from the sea, right? – asked Green.

- No, I am the stowaway – she smiled.

- To me you are the girl who came from the sea – stressed Green.

- I have no problem if you want to call me that, but my name is Nova.

- My name is Green, it is a pleasure to meet you

- You turn out to be my fan now – laughed Nova.

- It is just that I am very curious to know how you made it here, dodging all filters and securities - commented Green.

- Because I am a little bit of a rebel and like to break rules. When I get a "no", I always look for a "yes" – both laughed.

BREAKING THE RULES

They looked each other in the eye, and that same night they gave in to each other, without reservations, without accusations or blame, they became soul mates and they fused together without regrets.

Without them knowing, they have been united for life in a whisper. They contemplated the sea until sunrise, commenting on all the things lived. They promised to come back the next day. But the following day did not go as planned.

It was the longest day of the planet, an infinite silence ran rapidly throughout the sea. Sea currents stop flowing, the world stopped rotating. Minutes became hours for everyone and a big wave came over. Engines started to reach the deep end, you could see the fish being carried away unwillingly. The catastrophe had begun...

Nova Vida

Having gone through the worst of time and without having much time left to meditate on the catastrophe that took place everyone came together to bring forward what they believed to be their home.

Two months had passed since day Zero, and Nova was feeling a little bit strange. What appeared as side effects of a sickness turn out to be the best news for Dr. Green: Nova was pregnant.

The news took everyone by surprised since none of the Immune women could get pregnant. They were made infertile so that they could not get pregnant during their stay in the bunker or ships. They never thought of someone like

Nova, who never went through round of tests on the Immunes.

Everyone was feel with joy about the news of the baby, they took Nova and growing baby in her belly to celebrate that day.

The day for the baby to be born arrived, a day with excitement and anxiety, nobody expected the baby so early, only seven months into gestation and she already wanted to scream her lungs out to say that she was the first one of her species to be born in this new cycle of Axul. She was born with healthy lungs and her cry was heard all over the ship. She was the most expected baby ever. She brought new hope to Axulians. This was something that you did not see every day... They call her "Vida" (which means "Life").

Plan C: Orbiting Axul

After all the trajectories that took place from Axul to its satellites in the past, this time was different. This trip was the one that caused the biggest uncertainty because there were civilians aboard ship AXUL-S. Even though, what they wanted to do it was to orbit the planet on the side less exposed to Omega, the doubts and speculations raised as time passed. There was no ways to lower the possible harms that the solar radiation could cause on Axulians nevertheless, the hope of having a chance to keep the Axul race alive with this plan had not vanished... Even thou it seemed to them that this mission was the one that had more chances of survival, they still had to prove it...

Millionaires from all over planet Axul, famous people and

politicians bought their seats for this ship. The corruption was visible at all levels and people paid whatever the asking price was to have the opportunity of boarding the most secure ship that had been built (AXUL-S, next to AXUL-X)

People would bribe their way to the ship and to think that not even the entire wealth of the universe was worth such circumstances.

Some wealthy people could get their tickets on first row by trading their fortunes, but they could no longer count with bodyguards as they were accustomed to. They were not able to handle common chores well as the rest of passengers. They realized that their high class and royal personalities meant little or nothing aboard the ship. Soon they will give in and start to cooperate with the rest of the people.

Sand Gray was the daughter of a recently deceased business man and she inherited a seat on AXUL-S (Satellite). She knew everything regarding the last trends, but nothing about the basics of survival. She had grown up with all the luxuries money can buy but with a distant father. She was orphan of mother since young, she was raised by a nanny who she treated with great respect. The nanny helped her fill in the emptiness of her mother's absence and her father's indifference.

Considering that she had never worked in her life before, Sand was assigned as kitchen assistant. At her nineteen years of age she would truly understand what it really means to win her daily bread based on her own effort. After a while, she came to like the idea and at the end of the day she ate a piece of bread made by her own hands. She wasn't sure why or how, but it tastes like glory, the best that she had ever tasted in her entire life; so she took a piece for next morning's breakfast.

The following day, Sand was assigned to help wash the dishes.

PLAN C: ORBITING AXUL

With so many things to do, kitchen utensils, pots and pans she hadn't noticed how battered her hands were. After all that washing she looked at her hands and noticed that she had lost all brightness and softness, they had turned into rough hands. Another kitchen assistant had her eye on her. He didn't lose sight of her not even for a moment... He came close and took her hand without her noticing and said:

-   Do you know I can read your entire past on your hand? but for some reason I am not able to read your future. Because your future I see it reflected in your eyes, your future is me - and he smiled.

Sand acted up for a moment and removed her hand from his - but she still wanted to get to know him better. There were sparks or simple chemistry, something that attracted her to him without knowing what it was...

PLAN C: ORBITING AXUL

- Do I know you from somewhere? – Sand asked.
- Of course you do, but you don't remember it – Tadeu replied.
- I don't understand, where from? – she replied intrigued.
- From your dreams – as he turned around and walked away.

Tadeu was a single mother's child, he had been raised by his grandma and when it was possible his mom would visited him. Carmin who had to work hard to maintain both of them and their home, would take him on occasions to the place of work and it was then when he met Sand. He was eight years old when he saw her for the first time, she was six and they became inseparable from the get go, so much so that one of those few times he spent the night there. Sand's father noticed it and he did not approve of their friendship. He called Carmin and told her what he thought about it, making her promised that this will not happen again if she wanted to keep her job.   That was the last time Tadeu saw Sand personally until now.   She being "royalty" and all, it was inevitable for him to not read up about her on the socialite gossip column.

Reuniting with Sand filled him with joy and hope. He always felt something special for her... During all this time, it was his habit to ask his mom when he will see Sand again, and now just as if it was their destiny they had reunited once again. Perhaps this time they would be able to recover the forbidden loving friendship of those years.

The following day his eyes betrayed him again. He was captivated by her, she had that effect on him, he tried to not be so obvious about it, but this time Sand realize what was happening and she didn't look down once. She wanted to know who was behind those intense dark eyes that gave her the chills. Dragged by magnetism or something else, they came together and they felt like their feet were no longer

PLAN C: ORBITING AXUL

touching ground and everything flowed magically right.

In a moment Tadeu had told her everything about him. Who he really was and why he knew so much about her. They remembered their childhood memories and were trying to catch up on each other's lives when a big explosion was heard and then silence... It was a short beam of light in space which came to be a star dust traveling in time.

Plan D: Re-population of Planet Nev

This solution would only be temporary; it will be like gaining time while trying to find another Galaxy or a young Stellar System that contained an Exo-Planet.

The idea to create electromagnetic poles in Nev has been considered, this has already been done in Axul laboratories successfully. It only needed to be done on a bigger scale and implemented into the planet Nev, which happens to be very rich in Iron. This will be an advantage, since it would be like a dynamo with an attraction force strong enough to create an atmosphere. This could be achieved by implementing green houses that allow trees to exhale their oxygen during the day and to gather up the CO_2 during the night, that way optimum conditions could be in place to create a complete planet to

PLAN D: RE-POPULATION OF PLANET NEV

live on.

The only thing that was making them to rethink this escape plan would be that it would take so many years to accomplish it and they wouldn't know if they had enough time to make it happen. Would this only stay on paper?

Plan E: Voyage to another Stellar System

In AXUL-X they knew before hand that the trip would be without return. They couldn't take the privilege of making any mistakes. They needed to make sure everything would work as planned, that resources used such as oxygen, water food, etc. could be transformed and recycled to create a biological cycle without end to be mindful of the environment.

They had not found an Exo-Planet yet, the closest to them could be light years away in distance... How could they get there and live to tell the story? And how to know if this planet is habitable or not?

They needed to take this unavoidable risk, so they continue to scan the universe to find that perfect planet. A planet that can have all characteristics to support life, should have a perfect combination of oxygen, hydrogen, carbon and all the other elements to create the environment they were looking for.

They used huge telescopes and latest gadgets to scan all angles of the universe. They sent exploratory artifacts to find new worlds with signs of life, of hope... They realized this was a never ending task. They felt as if they were in a whirl wind of possibilities. What they were able to see from their stellar system was not the whole universe, but a fraction of it. In other words, they realized they were in a hole in the universe called Cronos... This stellar system was surrounded by a wall of fumes that made impossible to see beyond it...

Collapsing Barriers

They needed to start from scratch, from zero. Even though their proyections were with neighboring planets in the past, the idea of leaving planet Axul has never entered their minds until now, to leave their nest, to leave their homes, it was something they were not prepared for, something so unconceivable, something they would have never confronted before until destiny didn't give another option.

At last, the exploration systems scanning the universe found a signal coming from the opposite side of the galaxy. They were intelligent signs. Everyone was in awe with all the information they were able to gather. The information that came in not only with sounds, but also with videos and pictures. All were crying, clapping, laughing. They were filled with joy. They had found an inhabited planet called "Earth". Intelligent beings live there and they called themselves "Humans".

After this great news, they focused on how to get there. They have a new dilemma now... How are they planing to travel there?

- Worm Hole
- Asteroid APOPHIS[5]

Worm Hole: They speculated about the possibility to create a worm hole to travel there quickly. But this idea was rejected after realizing that there was not enough strong energy to create it.

Asteroid APOPHIS: As soon as they knew that Exo-Planet was close in orbit with Asteroid Apophis they made the

---

[5] **APOPHIS:** Asteroid that will be passing by Earth on 2029

decision to travel there to find their new home.

Earth was found on the way to Apophis, in a stellar system that Axulians called "Hope". Somehow, someway nobody knew for sure the asteroid joined together planet Axul and planet Earth as if knowing that someday they would need each other.

Apophis would be coming by planet Axul on it cyclical motion at any moment now, they would use this opportunity the asteroid is giving them to get to this fantastic and distant world.

Flight Logbook

The desired to fight for global peace was left far behind. At the end of times there was nothing left for anyone. There were no winners or defeated, it had been made clear that the times of war were only wasted time. They promised themselves that in this new created social system the fights for power will be only part of a dark past. Something that they would rather not remember. Their focus is in the common welfare of the people and the survival of their race.

They had to go through these apocalyptic events to learn from suffered experiences that now that they have so little, they have enough. Enough to find a new life, a new destiny, which must be handwritten, worked on and faced daily to achieve the set goals.

It caught my attention, a particular story that occurred during the travel of the ship AXUL-X. Everything spun around Savia and Silver, the young scientist who had warned about Axul's ending.

Savia was another AXUL-X passenger. She was deep in thought about all the things that the future may hold for her. With so many questions in her mind she didn't notice Silver who was seated next to her:

- Hello, how are you? – Asked Savia to Silver.
- Not too well right now – replied Silver.
- Yes, I know – Savia said – No one ever thought that after all we had to leave our Mother Planet. I know now how animals feel when their territory is taken from them.
- That's right – replied Silver.
- My name is Savia – She said.
- I'm Silver – He answered in a less shady mood than before.

FLIGHT LOGBOOK

By that time they had left Axul's orbit and gravity wasn't felt on their feet, but on their heads; everything was spinning around. It felt as if they had taken some type of drug, regardless they would have to start adapting.

Everyone was called through the speakers to gather and to be in their proper place in the ship, a capsule-bed which wasn't bigger than a coffin. Anyone who was claustrophobic would have to experience the worst of their fears. These capsules opened automatically letting out a bed that would ft comfortably. Normally the feet were towards the outer window of the ship, but Savia enjoyed being illuminated by the stars so much that she positioned herself in the opposite direction.

Silver and Savia became really good friends, every morning he went to the Scientist's cabin. A privilege mind she thought to herself. Savia on the other hand had tested positive for "Immune" , so she became an apprentice at the green houses.

The green houses had enough water and fertilizer and everything was done by a machine. She only had to give it the coordinates and timing for the different species of plants.

This position wasn't hard at all. In planet Axul she was a sower, in fact she came from a family of sowers. She had a particular scent about her. It is a good pleasant smell, the scent of rain on dry earth, as if she had tattooed a perfume of clay in her body, a scent that had become engraved on her skin throughout the years. Who would have thought that in the ship she would be assign the same job as the one she grew up with. She thanked destiny for it. She felt in a way reunited with her roots. She forced herself to believe that this place represented Axul's soul and that made her happy.

By lunch time she joined the entire personnel of her area and shared an extraordinary time. Besides the regular food, they had to take a hand full of vitamins pills to replace vitamin D, calcium, etc., nobody liked such diet but they couldn't complain to the chef. The only good thing about all this was the beautiful friendships gained, making the pills easier to take. After all, there is nothing better than a good conversation between friends.

APOPHIS

The time to land on APOPHIS had finally arrived, the ship had to be maneuvered very slowly to not hit the front but to land the best way possible to avoid any crash.

Savia went near a window, her hazel eyes saw when the ship landed on the asteroid feeling safer then, just like when you buy a train ticket knowing what would be the next stop. She also felt as if the huge rock gave her hope of a new home.

As she stared at APOPHIS, she sensed somebody looking over her shoulders, thru the glassy window she saw a silhouette, it was Silver. He came near looking at her like never before. A deep sadness overtook him. Hopelessness invading his inner being. He dropped to her feet and burst out crying as a baby in a sea of tears.

- What's wrong Silver? – She asked kneeling next to him (Silver didn't speak only hugged her tighter).
- You can count on me Silver, tell me what is going on? – She asked again.
- We have lost contact with the AXUL-S space craft; everything indicates that there is nothing left – replied Silver.

They were speechless, thick tears ran down their cheeks, and they couldn't stop thinking of anything else but their family members.

If only there had been more ships, if there were closer planets to go to, if they had found this out sooner they asked themselves.

They didn't know that the Axulians from AXUL-B and AXUL-Z were still alive, but once the satellite was lost, they thought that nobody had survived.

The Axulians on the ship were devastated, nothing made sense anymore. Desolated and frightened they were once again doubting their chances of survival.

In her sadness however, Savia started to feel that they still had a purpose. She was not going to allow sadness to overcome her hope, dreams, goals. On the contrary, that the ones left behind had to be the motivation and strength for them to continue forward and not to give up.

Somehow in the midst of all kind of emotions Savia stood up, helping Silver do the same. She gave him more than a shoulder to cry on, she gave him hope. Hope that things will get better, that they will make it, and that they will overcome the biggest obstacles they have ever had, and to continue with the legacy of an entire race, and to prevail no matter what problems come their way. She held his face and pointed it towards the outside of the window to APOPHIS and said:

APOPHIS

- What do you see Silver?
- APOPHIS? – He replied.
- Don't you think it's beautiful – Savia continued (Silver didn't reply only nodded).
- Then enjoy the moments that life gives you. Look at what's in front of you, and what is yet to come. Find your purpose in life and you will get the meaning of it. Don't let the past bury you along with it. Live the present thinking of a future to build. Memories are good as long as they don't consume you – confirmed Savia.

He looked at her face to face, with a blurry sight and a little bit calmer and he said:

- Thank you for your words, they have given me strength in one of the most critical moments of my life, you are absolutely right, I can see my horizon clearer now and what I have to do - concluded Silver.

He kissed her forehead and left without looking back, he had to re-order his ideas and clear his thoughts.

The next day Savia woke up a little later than usual. It felt to her as if a thousand years had passed by. Having only taken just a few footsteps the sound alarms started to go off. Everyone rushed to their assigned seats, it was the procedure. She could feel panic overtaking her emotions, adrenaline rushed thru her veins and her heart started to beat faster. Somehow she managed to get to her seat.

Silver was looking all over for her and when he didn't find her on her cubicle he ran to the navigational seat. He found her there, feeling happy in seeing her; he explained what was going on:

- We are passing through the "K-PLUM BELT" and there is the possibility that some meteorites will impact the ship – Silver assured.
- When will this happen? – asked Savia.

- Now! – Silver replied as he held her hand and in a whirlwind of emotions they embraced each other…

It was then that Savia felt something stronger than gravity in her pupils. Something more powerful than anything else she had ever experienced before. She let herself take in this emotion that swept her off her feet. She lost consciousness a second later after the first meteor impacted the ship.

There were five meteors in total that impacted the ship but only two relatively big enough to cause damage, which was fixed as soon as the "K-PLUM BELT" was crossed.

Silver woke her up with a soft touch on her face, she could feel the softness and warmth of his hands. There was no doubt to both of them that love has overwhelmed their souls, they understood it as is.

Silver was called immediately over the speakers to the

command cabin. They had to implement a new anti-risk plan in case this happened again; they couldn't afford to expose themselves to another meteor rain.

That same night Silver went to meet Savia, she was seating down on her cubicle reading a very antique book which still had its cover intact. As if someone hadn't read it in years, a cultural treasure for sure. One of those books that had been extinct a long time ago. She had kept it with such a sentimental value for so long, since her grandfather gave it to her as a child; the book was named: "From love and other emotions".

She paused as soon as she saw Silver through the window and she rushed to meet him. She had waited all day for this moment though she had no idea on what to do or say. She approached him as if something drew her to his arms and for the first time she felt the strength in them. She didn't doubt for a second and looked at him with tenderness as if asking for mercy and said:

- Getting loss in your eyes is of great gain in my life – She said to him.
- I love you Silver, and I wouldn't know what to do without you – continued Savia.

Silver stared at her intensely as if wanting to beat time to gain minutes from it, he kissed her as if it was the first and last kiss he would ever give her.

- I love you Savia- Silver smiled - you have given my life sense. You have brought light to my darkness and I don't care what happens as long as I know you also love me. I have already achieve eternity with you.
- There is something I have to tell you - Silver made a pause - We don't know how long this trip is going to take, so we are all being taken to the hibernation

capsules until we have entered the "Hope system". These capsules have all the vitamins and nutrients to sustain life, they are programmed for that. I had asked to be placed on close capsules because the first thing I want to see when waking up is your eyes. I don't want to be away from you, with you I feel alive.

At that moment she took his hand and guided him to her cubicle, it was a bit narrow but it didn't matter. It only took them a second to realize that their love was the closest to eternity that they could ever be.

"His eyes caught mine, his skin aligned with mine, he took me by the hand and we became in essence, one"...Savia

All passengers of the ship were called through speakers to go to their seats in the auditorium; they told them what was going to happen, this time they had to form lines in order to be assigned to their hibernation chambers. Without being able to complain or state their opinions, everyone headed to their chambers, it just wasn't the best time for doubts.

Silver and Savia were helping everyone until the very last, giving out information and placing them where they needed to be. It was the last time to see themselves as they were, just how Silver had planned Savia's eyes were the last thing he looked at. At that moment he began to feel a cold liquid covering him, it felt as if their bodies were being frozen. The light turned off and the deepest dream overtook their bodies. Their souls leaving them, and just like an astral travel he found himself standing out of his physical body. He then realized he could see through his hands because he was transparent, and what had been an enigma became clear.

Astral Life

He saw her standing there, her soul above her body. She was trying to coordinate ideas and she was also thinking that everything was a dream. Silver who had already incorporated and accepted it's new self was trying to make Savia understand that they weren't just bodies but souls as well hat they were united by an unexplainable link and without measuring words they say so much to each other that it didn't feel so strange after all. It was a pilgrim moment, one of those you feel for the first time and without much thought you ending up accepting it. They were on a different phase of existence now, a stated that only people with near death experiences are able to understand. After all, death is only a transition from a physical life to a spiritual one, where the souls transcends from one state to another, since the body has a soul and also a spirit, which eternity could never take away.

ASTRAL LIFE

There are situations in which our reasoning isn't always correct, nor do we have all the right answers, but it is with the heart that one sees what is impossible to see with the naked eye.

Everyone in the ship had the same extrasensory experience, and after that instant, it was no longer necessary to talk to understand each other because they were able to do so telepathically if they wanted to. Without looking for it they found a way of communicating without a voice.

Thoughts are electric pulses and just as on Earth, Alexander Graham Bell discovered the sending of voice through phones, something similar must have taken place with the thoughts.

Since they had been hibernating while traveling on the asteroid APOPHIS, they didn't realize when the ship entered the solar system. It was only when the ship's computer started to depressurize all the hibernation chambers that they were able to came out of it, and in a way, they were born again.

The feeling that they had was as if a hundred years turned into a day and then everyone woke up.

A New Awakening

The first thing that Savia felt was Silver's hand, nothing could have made her happier, being reborn in his sight was a gift from life, everything blossomed around her. It could be compared to a newborn seeing the light for the first time. Savia was not able to recognize Silver, but some how she knew it was him. His physical appearance had changed, but his soul was still there. The gentle way he would look at her made Savia not to notice the little details on his appearance that at the end weren't important.

Due to the hibernation process and the time that they were in the fluids chambers to maintain them alive during this trip, their scales were lost. Their skin had changed color and they were paler than before. They had loose skin folds all over their bodies due to the massive weight and muscular mass loss. The one thing they had preserved were their eyes, a predominant feature on the Axulians. Their eyes were big and round and different colors but always with the astonished look that they will never lose.

- How are you? – Silver said.
- Alright – Savia replied – missing you.

Silver didn't stare at the bags under her eyes, or baldness or new wrinkles but her heart.

- Would you like to have a family with me? – Silver asked.
- I would love too – Savia replied, a bit surprised and looking at those sky eyes.

They both smiled feeling complete and happy to know they have each other. Even though they had lost everything, they knew bigger and better things will come their way.

"Hope" Stellar System

As I had previously explained our stellar system was called "Hope" by the Axulians, it was the best name they could give it. It was their new hope and now it didn't seem so far.

They sent space waves to dig for information of each planet in this stellar system. There was a total of nine planets, in which they found there was only one that had the same distance to the Sun similar to Axul and its star Omega and it was habitable. They had found it earlier and seeing it so close only made them want to know more about it. It would be the third planet called "Earth". They would hold onto it so tight as a baby would hold onto life when born with their first cry, as earth holds life after the first rain of spring.

With an atmosphere similar to theirs, "Earth" could host them, keep them warm, but they didn't know if human beings will allow them to stay.

As they traveled to the interior of the Solar system, they discovered by chance a black hole. In the far horizon farther than the Cronos system, even farther than the Galaxy's limit, this black hole was creating planets and stars that would become new systems and galaxies. This was a new spark of knowledge in their lives. They knew how everything started in this universe, and there wasn't just one but many universes and black holes.

They came to the conclusion that it all depends if the black hole expelled or swallowed matter. If the black hole expelled matter is considered to be a "Generator" of new universes, if it swallowed matter it is a "Destroyer" of them. On the long run "Destroyers" will become "Generators" but on a different stellar plane.

"HOPE" STELLAR SYSTEM

After this, new theories came up. There were some who suggested that when two galaxies crash an enormous explosion of such strength takes place, destroying dark matter (which separate us from other universes). At that point is when black holes are created. Their attraction force is so big that nothing would escape from being devoured in its way and the entire cycle starts again...

After new discoveries, and the time they were hibernating, they started to get used to their new bodies and environment. They returned to their daily activities and responsibilities with renewed strength. They had overcome another survival test, and everyone felt optimistic. They believed what seems impossible can be made possible and that everything will be ok when they arrive on planet Earth.

There were times when Silver, as the Scientist that he was, had thousands of ruminating thoughts going on in his mind:

"What would happen if instead of oxygen they had methanol or any toxic gas in their atmosphere?"

"What would happen if the weather is too hostile to stay in it?"

He tried to avoid these ruminating thoughts and to stay positive, after all they had gone through, he knew one way or another they always went forward.

Silver tried to stay focus on work, but doubts plagued his mind. Just thinking about Savia changed his moods, his eyes sparkled and he could see things clearer. He felt safe when she was next to him, he went looking for her:

- Silver what are you doing here at this time? – Savia asked – (and even though he had never gone to her work place she loved the surprise).
- I came to check out your world and soak up from you – He said taking her hands.

She got a little nervous pushing buttons without realizing... An unexpected shower soaked them as they began to laugh, finishing off with a hug.

- This will be your smell – Silver said – the one who will keep me company for a thousand lives, and it will always be you that comes to my mind in every random shower.

It was a mix of smells from all the flowers together, from all the plants together, that smell of soaking wet dirt that translated him to his origins.

- Because all my paths lead to you – continued Silver – even if you change faces or bodies I will always find you.

He took her in his arms forgetting for a moment where they were. He kissed her without caring about the rain or the people there, believing for a moment to be invisible...

They felt surrounded by voices, whispers and giggles of their fellow workers. They became conscious of their surroundings... Savia blushed and ran away...

"She left, leaving me her scent. I already missed her"...Silver

With Saturn in their hands

They were about to pass close to Saturn. Silver wanted to give Savia this surprise since she had never seen a planet with rings, let along it be so close. He knew she would love it so he couldn't let the moment spoil. He took her to the stellar portal balcony which had the biggest windows of the ship, taking her with a blindfold.

- I want you to see something – Silver said.
- If you are going to play a joke on me I need to know what I'm getting myself into – She said with an accomplice smile.

When she opened her eyes, she saw the majesty and beauty of that planet. She placed her hand on the glass window as if wanting to touch it. Her astonishment was so big that she was speechless. She was like that for a while until she felt Silver's hand on hers. She looked at him and a tear of happiness captured that moment.

- It's the best present I've ever received in my life – Savia said.
- It is truly beautiful, when I saw it immediately thought of you – replied Silver.

Savia looked at him with love, gently touched his face, placing her forehead on his, and then leaning her head on his shoulder; they both stared at Saturn. Savia asking him what its name was and what was it made of.

- Humans know it as Saturn and its atmosphere is made up of gas, the rings have formed from several residues, probably caused by asteroids or comets collisions – answered Silver.

WITH SATURN IN THEIR HANDS

-   A lot of time must have passed to take this form –
    Savia mentioned – this is spectacular!

After crossing Saturn they felt as if the asteroid had sped up its trajectory, as is APOPHIS knew it was carrying a very valuable cargo and to keep its hosts with hope. The Axulians had become so attached to this piece of rock that had been a transit place for them, a forced stop to follow the path. A path that will bring them closer to their new life in a world so distant and magical at the same time.

Arriving to Earth
(Year 2029 Planet Earth)

They showed up on a sunny day in March, it was Sunday in a location called "Tamarind", at the valley of a town near the ocean, somewhere along the Equatorial line.

Everyone on Earth was terrified to see something they hadn't seen before. Even though, they had always speculated about extraterrestrial life, seeing how majestic their ship was only made their fear grow. Panic took over the people, as it started to descend the fear grew stronger. But curiosity was bigger and the desire to know what was going on made a mob of people gather around the UFO.

They landed in an old airport which had already been forgotten about. Within moments AXUL-X was surrounded by so many people that they could hardly see what was farther. It was a sea of people and as the time went by more people arrived. Police officers, fire fighters, news people and even the army was present, covering the entire area.

I was still inside the ship, they asked me to please help them as their translator. Although they could easily read human minds, they didn't want to frighten anyone. So I became their official translator until the complete bondage and adaptation can take place on planet Earth.

The community of nations soon met up, they had to make decisions about the new events. They decided to meet at "Tamarind". They needed to know what the situation was in case they came in a conquering mode.

Inside the ship everything was happiness, they were astonishment to see a different species of intelligent life. Even though they already knew some of us to see that amount of human beings was like a big gasp of hope, they had made it, so many emotions together, and so little time to convince their earth siblings to let them stay.

In the short time that I had been with Axulians I already care so much about them. They were pacific beings wanting a chance to survive, and if I could help them stay I would do it, so I offered myself to be the first one to come out of the ship.

They opened the doors and I started to come out of it, everyone stared at me as if I was from another planet or something else. Why were they predisposed to think like that? I approached the mediators ready to negotiate and introduced myself. I let them know who I was and why I was inside.

- Hello my name is Eidan S. Laiton. I am Human and I was chosen to be the official translator between the Axulians inside the ship and us Human Beings... - I continued

- They come from the other side of the galaxy, from a planet in destruction named Axul which belongs to the Cronos Stellar System. They just need a place to stay.

At first they were surprised to hear me speak in perfect English, but as I kept talking about their story it created a more relaxed atmosphere. Only then it was known Axulians had come in peace. They just wanted a chance to stay, and start to adapt to the new environment.

A meeting took place, and the board members of the community of nations were ready to go inside the ship one by one. They started to come in though they were scared to death, their protocol prohibited them to show their emotions. There were so many questions to be had, a crucial question was made:

- How did you know there was life on Earth? – asked the Secretary of the Community Nations

- We could see your signals on the cropped corn circles – I answered on their behalf as they scroll those images on the main screen. Fig. 5
- What are you talking about? – Expressed the Secretary – those circles have not been done by Human hands.

So then, who did them? Was the question that everyone had in the room, which left new questions in the air...

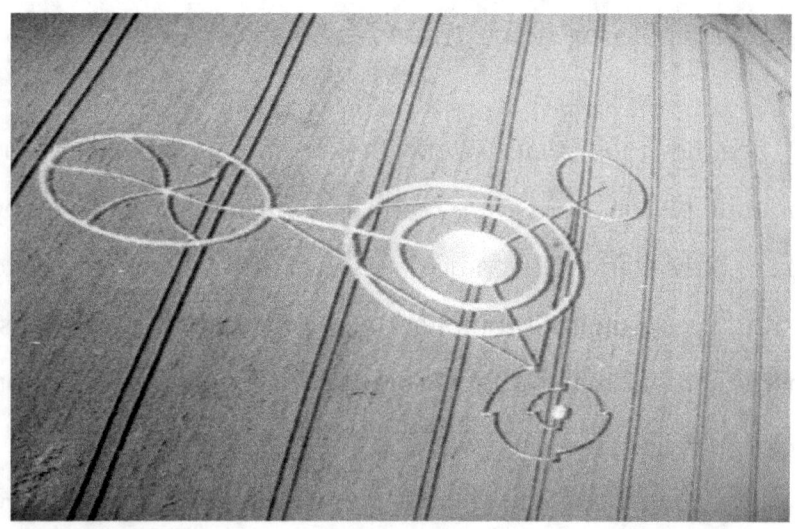

Fig. 5

PART TWO

A Home to build

The community of nations and the principal members of Axul decided that they needed to talk more in details to figure this out. What could the cropped corn maze signals meant? Also they needed to decide which place on Earth the Axulians would occupy.

Negotiations continued as nations didn't want to give up their territories, they had no clue as to where to re-locate them. An extremist commissioner suggested sending them to the Antarctic. There was silence in the entire room, they started to whisper, talk between teeth and about the possibility of sending them there.

I asked myself, how can human beings be so cruel?

A HOME TO BUILD

Where is our humanity? Where is our compassion for others? When did we lose that human part of helping those in need?

It seemed so unfair to send them to the ends of the world, where plants don't blossom, where life will be really hard to sustain due to the freezing cold temperatures. I let them know how I felt about it, but they were accusing me of interrupting negotiations, to them I was just the translator. Crion looked at me and sent me a message that soothed me, they paused the discussion and called it a break.

I was feeling really disappointed in myself for not being able to help more. Crion knew exactly how I felt, telling me telepathically to not worry, that they will follow any command, they weren't here to create new wars but to survive, to adapt to any environment regardless of how hostile it could be. So they settled in Antarctic. They realized soon enough that it will be a challenge to settle there, but they had no choice, no other option. Since they could not appeal the decision they accepted their new home.

The Axulians started to make plans to build in Antarctica domes just how they had on their planet. It will help them during the assimilation process and somehow it will make them feel at home.

They scanned the entire continent of Antarctica with their ship. They were surprised to discover old ruins from a lost civilization in the frozen continent. As stated in the law they reported this new discovery to the terrestrial authorities. An investigative unit was formed, Axulians and Humans who will work together in the excavation process. All sorts of materials and machinery began to arrived. Even with such horrid weather the excavations didn't stop, they wanted to speed up the discovery of a lost city.

Little by little, it started to take shape. A sunken ghost town under ice. It's discovery began to give life to a myth. Buried eighty meters under snow where hidden structures of outrageous dimensions. So big that they seemed to have been built for, and by giants. These people were smart enough to have their own written language on the walls of monuments.

It wasn't just coincidence that within the work group there was an Egyptian archaeologist who helped with the translation of the writings on the wall.

"A monument dedicated to pushing
the Atlantis town forward"

What had seemed to be a myth, a legend for so long, it would become part of the history of planet Earth.

Axulians also helped to confirm that there was a time on Earth when the South Pole went through a meltdown, or a period in which it was over sea level. The reason being was that this part of the Earth was exposed to the sun for too long. It

A HOME TO BUILD

means Earth had only two seasons, while in the South Pole was summer for a long time, in the North Pole was winter for the same time. From there, the theory of the ice age was confirmed, but only for the North Pole during these circumstances.

With such contributions, confirmations and scientific discoveries to planet Earth, Humans understood that the new comers weren't there to take things away, but to help with science and technology advances. From that day on, Humans saw them with new eyes, they created new immigration laws to allow them not just to stay on planet Earth, but also to help new generations to seen them as equals. Once and for all they were welcome to move free on planet Earth, it could be called now "Human Planet".

Crop circles

Alternatively, they had called up an urgent meeting of scientists with a mission: "to reveal the crop circles"

There was an entrepreneurship developing, a constant search to resolve the paradigms of planet Earth. With priority to the crop circles. They knew that whoever made these crop circles must have an intelligence mind, perhaps had the key to many unsolved mysteries, not just for planet Earth but Axul's as well.

Out of all crop corn circles that had been collected over the years, they chose two that were absolutely complex on their designs.

In between the crop circle there was one that got their attention "The Triada". Fig.6

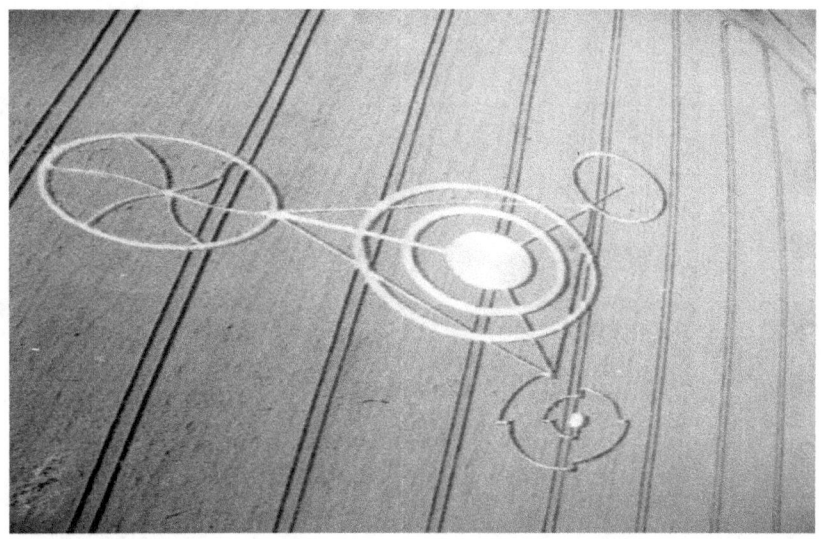

In this picture, we are able to see three different stellar systems. Our solar system on the West, Cronos on the South and an empty system and not explored on the North-East. The black hole of our galaxy is represented as the center. It is believed that from this hidden stellar system located on the North-East is where the crop circles come from. But why is it empty? This is what we need to find out.

Another circle that also had gotten our attention was "The
Theory of the Descend" Fig. 7

This image practically represents the stellar system Cronos
and its first four planets.

It couldn't be done by a person without extensed math
knowledge or notion of space. Who can be responsible for
this? It could be an astronomer, a mathematician or a more

advanced mind than from our time. The truth is in the message that they want to give us. The planets are placed as if they are balls on a pinball machine, every external circle represents an orbit. The filled circles represent the planets on those orbits. When that planet comes down to an inferior orbit, after some time in space, it repeats doing so until it gets to Omega which is in the middle. The little point on the second orbit is nothing more than the planet Solenoid entering on the closest orbit to its star Omega.

There was still plenty to resolve. A new space craft had to be built to discover who the crop circles authors were and why they had guided them there.

Among humans, a young lady stood out, a scientist on the astronomy field, a fresh mind and new ideas that may be of help on the search of this new stellar system. Her name: "Sara Smith"

CROP CIRCLES

Although she wasn't going to travel on the spacecraft. She could help discover the hidden messages in the circles. The one that would travel on the craft was her boyfriend: Mikhail. The crew will be a mix of the ones who already traveled to earth and new human explorers.

They will travel through the "Dark Rift" because going through a black hole wasn't the best idea, not possible, since the gravity and pressure would destroy the ship with everyone inside. The Dark Rift gave them a chance to explore the darkest side of the galaxy and even though humans had never gone that far, this time they were ready to do so, if they have a chance to find the answers to their doubts.

The trip would be done on the south summer of the following year. This way they will have plenty of time to finish building the new space ship.

TERA-X

The new space ship was called TERA-X. It was finished during the expected time. Tools and design were the same as the ones used to built Axul's crafts, but this one on a smaller scale. In Antarctica humans were so excited. A new era of discoveries had started and they couldn't wait.

Mikhail invited Sara to an unexpected journey, and although the polar cold wasn't the best environment, there was no ice that a hot heart couldn't melt. They stole a snow machine and went away in search of adventure. They walked thru a desolated road where no life could be seen on the horizon. They setup camp and started a bonfire. Mikhail took a letter out of his shirt pocket close to his heart. It was his way of saying goodbye.

"The look in your eyes are like the ocean blue,

from afar I perceived them salty,

and even though I will draw your words daily,

I long to hear them from your lips...

then you will come out of nothing

with the north wind,

you will cuddle up from the cold under my wings,

from this embrace sparks will come out

to light up the color of your eyes...

to your passion I hold on to

your scent transcends my senses

I get away from this world to end up on your lap,

a life, a moment, a waking up with you".

They could see the midnight sun in that corner of the world
where the moon is elusive and the sun never hides.

Second Voyage

(July 2030 Planet Earth)

On a July morning everything was ready for the take-off and the space ship passed through the infinite sky.

Mikhail and Crion became good friends, the one thing that was out of limits for Crion was to pick on his mind. Advice that Crion took heed to because he was a gentleman rather than prohibition itself.

Everyone in the space craft was aware that perhaps this will be a one way trip. This time there was no asteroid to help them in their journey, only a crop circle map and willingness.

The Dark Rift was like a secret passage, a direct portal to where they wanted to go. It took three years to get the other side. It was a dark place of the galaxy, like a twilight zone. They arrived to a semi-hidden stellar system with a star that was almost ready to be extinguished. In astronomy they are called "White dwarf stars". Usually they are stars that have used up their energy and no longer produce the same heat as the first days; practically just another stellar remnant.

When they got closer they were finally able to recognize this system. It was known as "The Eye of God". Fig. 8

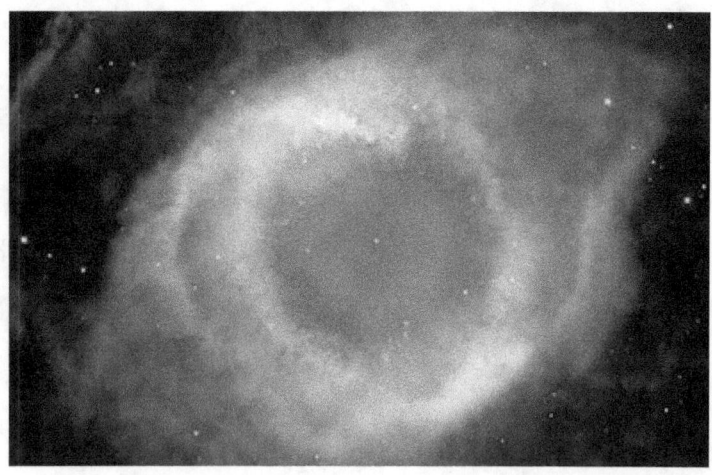

SECOND VOYAGE

They scanned the system to see if there was any form of life in this dark place.

They found the Silencers, beings that would shine with their own lights. In other words, their radiance bodies were shining reflections of a non-burning light taken from their sun "Torch".

The temperature of this planet was so cold, that they had to use special resistant suits to get out.

They had human shape with metallic structures and regardless they could move around naturally.

Just like the Axulians, the Silencers communicated telepathically, but their perception range was wider and longer. They manipulate the infrared waves easily. They didn't speak cause the volume of their voice was so strong that they could make everyone go deaf and faint. If you have ever heard the train rail tracks sound when breaking, you may have a slight idea of how Silencers may sound, multiplying that to the tenth power.

Their bodies based on silicon (semi-metal, element 14), were rough on the outside, but noble on the inside. From their planet "Silence" they sent the Axulians warnings signs of danger. Using the Earth as a mirror to create the cropped circles signals, which were detected from Axul.

Metamorphosis

Helio Von Engels a young adventurer Silencer volunteer to visit Earth. A Silencers diplomatic group would also travel to create: "Allied League Zonal of Stellar Organizations" (ALZSO).

ALZSO would be the organization responsible to maintain peace, cooperation, integration and respect between stellar systems.

Once inside the ship, while traveling back to planet Earth, Axulians and Humans started to notice the metamorphosis of the Silencers. Their body shapes started to transform to liquid, like water in a plastic container. Silencers explained to them all that depending on the temperature of where they are their physical appearance changes.

During the trip an environment of happiness filled the place; there was peace, security and trust, worthy of intelligent beings. Mikhail was counting the days down to see Sara; there was so much he wanted to share with her, and a question to ask.

It took a little over three years to return back to Earth. In mid-January they were landing at "Tamarind" base. Helio with his innocent personality was the first one to go out. He came out running, trying to get to know the new world. But he didn't know it would be at a high risk.

The high Ecuadorian temperatures evaporated his immortal soul, turning him into gas that dispersed into the wind.

Inside the ship nobody could believe their eyes, their hearts sank and everyone expressed their pain in their own way.

Crion could not accept the death of his new friend and will do even the impossible to find out what happened to him.

This incident made them take extra precautions with the rest of the crew. They were placed in quarantine (for three days). They had to be extra careful transporting the rest of Silencers to the Axul base in the South Pole. Perhaps, in this extreme temperature they will feel as if they are in their planet "Silence" and return to their metallic shape.

A few days later Crion had a video conference with Silver, explaining what had happened to Helio.

"They say that on cold nights they can see his silhouette around the airport"...Crion

Helio had become an urban legend, a ghost that didn't scare anyone, but couldn't be taken out of that gas stage. Silver thought about "Memory of metals".

METAMORPHOSIS

$$S=(PxV)^6$$

Silver went to Ecuador and it's "0" latitude, with Crion and Mikhail's help he joined in forces to help Helio out. Just like true ghost busters, they went through the airport centimeter by centimeter. A soft wind brushed their faces, it had to be definitely him. Silver turned the vacuum on to catch the gas. As if he was a genie in a bottle, they took him to the South Pole.

During the time Mikhail was in space, on Earth Sara had an accident at the age of 25. This accident left her in a deep coma, Doctors transported her to a cryogenic chamber. Three years had passed and with the evolution of science a miracle took place. Her brain was re-implanted in a cyber-body that returned her back to life.

---

6   S= Temperature Constant; P= Pressure; V= Volume

She then, continued her life on the science field at Axul's main base and one day she had been notified the return of "TERA-X". The exploring shuttle in which Mikhail had traveled.

She was so excited, but she also had her doubts. Thinking if Mikhail would accept her current form. She went to see him, but he didn't notice her in her new shape. He even walked next to her, but she let him pass by and turned her head down. She felt that she was crying, tears wouldn't come out... She decided to wait a bit longer to meet him. She was very emotional at the moment.

Crion, Mikhail and Silver went to a cold temperature laboratory chamber located in the Axul's base where Helio was kept. They put the capsule on a bigger chamber and proceeded to open it. They lower the temperature and soon as they did that you could see Helio's outline once again. All his voyage friends were there to congratulated him. For Crion and Mikhail this was more than just a change from gas to solid, it was more like from sad to overjoyed time. Helio also smiled. During the voyage they had created a beautiful bond of brotherhood, just like the three modern musketeers. They had so much trust with each other that they even got nicknames. They called each other: monkey[7], chimera[8] and aluminum foil[9]. It made me laugh how they treated each other.

Sara was waiting outside the laboratory and this time she faced him head on and called him by his name:

- "Mikhail" – She yelled (but held still to not hug him, she didn't want to scare him).
- Do I know you? – replied Mikhail surprised.
- I'm Sara – She replied.

He stared at her firmly trying to recognize her in that body.

---

[7] **Monkey:** Because of Darwin's theory
[8] **Chimera:** Because of the fish Chimera
[9] **Aluminum foil:** Because of its semi-metallic composition

METAMORPHOSIS

He was very surprised (and his friends left them alone).

- How can this be? This can't be – He said
- I know this may sound incredible, but I had an accident and they planted my brain on a Cyberbody – Sara replied.

After Sara explained what had happened to her he still couldn't believe this had taken place while he was gone. He took her hand and asked her:

- Can you feel this? – He asked, placing his hand over the palm of her artificial hand.
- No – She replied stuttering a bit - I don't have all the senses like smelling, taste, or touch, but I've discovered a new sense that we usually let pass by... The human sense, which is what makes me feel love, happy or sad. I know this is not something I can see or touch, but is part of me...

More than a feeling and emotions, it's to let out the best we have, our heart. It is with the heart that we feel the most beautiful and noble of feelings. This is what makes us "human beings"

Mikhail leaned close and whispered in her ear. In secret he said these numbers knowing she will understand[10]:

01001001

01001100

01001111

01010110

01000101

01010101

"ILOVEU, without space nor time, because the heart doesn't care what physics or chemistry not even what biology says... This is simply love" - Whispered Mikhail looking at her eyes.

---

[10] **Binary Code:** ILOVEU

METAMORPHOSIS

He kissed her hand, then he got teary eyes and he knew it was her. He didn't care how changed she was on the outside if knew her on the inside. Right then and there he asked her to marry him. It was the first time a man and a cyber-body will be married and that was just the beginning...

THE END

"I want to thank God

for guiding me when I couldn't see,

for healing me when I couldn't walk

and for loving me when I couldn't love"

Planet Axul is a science fiction book, with light traces of reality that make us question ourselves if there is something from the plot that couldn't be a parallel world with our planet Earth.

This book was created from the subconscious...
A dream crossed frontiers to land on my head and then to write it an almost exact way, something unreal, but at the same time too vivid...

Plenty of times we daydream
Wishing for better days,
Wanting that those dreams
Will become reality.
These dreams give us strength
And make us forge our destiny....

My dreams came without being called up
From a deep sleep
To fool my senses...

...Perhaps this dream will never become reality, but it turned into ideas...
to be born in: "Planet Axul"

Edition Thanks to:
Ines Velez
Esther Miller

English Translation Thanks to:
Maria Fernanda Miño
Mayara de los Santos

Photos Special Thanks to:
"God's Eye" – Helix Nebula by NASA
"The Triada" – Barbury Castle Crop Cir. 1991 by Richard Wintle
"Drop Theory" – Barbury Castle Crop Cir. 2008 by Lucy Pringle

www.planetaxul.com

www.ingramcontent.com/pod-product-compliance
Lightning Source LLC
Chambersburg PA
CBHW070557180626
46817CB00005B/1881